Nelson Readers
Series editor: Lewi[s]

A library of graded readers
reluctant native readers. Th[ese]
Structure, vocabulary, idio[m]
principles laid down in det[ail]
The books are listed below
300 words and appropriate
words, 5: 2000 words and [6]
accompanied by a cassette.

C000038571

Level Four

The White South *Hammond Innes*
A Christmas Carol *Charles Dickens*
King Solomon's Mines*
H Rider Haggard
Jane Eyre *Charlotte Brontë*
Pride and Prejudice *Jane Austen*
Dr Jekyll and Mr Hyde*
R L Stevenson
Huckleberry Finn *Mark Twain*
Landslide *Desmond Bagley*
Nothing is the Number When You Die
Joan Fleming
The African Child *Camara Laye*
The Lovely Lady and Other Stories
D H Lawrence
Airport International *Brian Moynahan*
The Secret Sharer and other Sea Stories
Joseph Conrad
Death in Vienna? *K E Rowlands*
Hostage Tower* *Alistair MacLean*
The Potter's Wheel *Chukwuemeka Ike*
Tina Turner *Stephen Rabley*
Campbell's Kingdom *Hammond Innes*
Barchester Towers *Anthony Trollope*
Rear Window *Cornell Woolrich*
Britain: The Inside Story *Lewis Jones*

Level Five

The Guns of Navarone
Alistair MacLean
Geordie *David Walker*
Wuthering Heights *Emily Brontë*
Where Eagles Dare *Alistair MacLean*
Wreck of the Mary Deare
Hammond Innes
I Know My Love *Catherine Gaskin*
The Mayor of Casterbridge
Thomas Hardy
Sense and Sensibility *Jane Austen*
The Eagle Has Landed *Jack Higgins*
Middlemarch *George Eliot*
Victory *Joseph Conrad*
Experiences of Terror* *Roland John*
The Freedom Trap *Desmond Bagley*

Level Six

Doctor Zhivago *Boris Pasternak*
The Glory Boys *Gerald Seymour*
In the Shadow of Man *Jane Goodall*
Harry's Game *Gerald Seymour*
House of a Thousand Lanterns
Victoria Holt
Hard Times *Charles Dickens*
Sons and Lovers *D H Lawrence*
The Dark Frontier *Eric Ambler*
Vanity Fair *William Thackeray*
Inspector Ghote Breaks an Egg
H R F Keating

Thomas Nelson and Sons Ltd
Nelson House, Mayfield Road
Walton-on-Thames, Surrey
KT12 5PL, UK

51 York Place
Edinburgh
EH1 3JD, UK

Thomas Nelson (Hong Kong) Ltd
Toppan Building 10/F
22a Westlands Road
Quarry Bay, Hong Kong

This edition © Lewis Jones 1979

First published by Collins ELT 1979

Reprinted: 1981, 1982, 1984, 1986, 1987, 1988, 1989, 1990

ISBN 0-00-370119-0

This edition first published by
Thomas Nelson and Sons Ltd 1992

ISBN 0-17-556573-2
NPN 9 8 7 6 5 4 3 2

We are grateful to BBC Copyright Photographs
for permission to reproduce the photograph
which appears on the cover.
Our thanks are also due to Anne Stallybrass and
Alan Bates for granting their permission.

Printed in Great Britain
by Bell and Bain Ltd., Glasgow

Nelson Readers Level 5

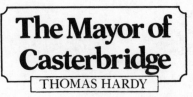

The Mayor of Casterbridge

THOMAS HARDY

Abridged and simplified by Lewis Jones

Nelson

1

One evening of late summer, before the nineteenth century had run a third of its course, a young man and woman were approaching the large village of Weydon-Priors on foot.

They were plainly but not badly dressed, though the thick powdery dust of an obviously long journey was no advantage to their appearance. The man was a fine figure. His short brown jacket was newer than the remainder of his suit. At his back he carried a basket, at one end of which stood out the handle of a knife for cutting hay.

The couple walked side by side in perfect silence. The wife was carrying a child, and she enjoyed no society whatever from the presence of the man. When she looked down sideways to the child, she became pretty, and even handsome. When she marched on in the sun, she had the hard expression of one who no longer expects fair play from Time or Chance.

When the houses of Weydon-Priors could just be seen in the distance, the family was met by a villager with a dinner-bag over his shoulder.

"Any trade here?" the man asked him. "Any

work with the hay?"

The villager had already begun shaking his head.

"Then is there any house to let – a little small new cottage just built or such-like?" said the other.

"Pulling houses down is more in the nature of Weydon than building them."

Distant sounds and laughter reached their ears from the village, and the husband waved a hand in that direction.

"There's something going on there, is there not?"

"Yes. 'Tis Fair Day. Though what you hear now is the noise of getting money away from children and fools. The real business was done earlier than this."

The husband and his family continued on their way, and soon entered the Fair-field, which showed standing-places where hundreds of horses and sheep had been sold before noon. Yet the crowd was thicker now than during the morning.

Our visitors looked for a refreshment tent among the many that stood on the green. In front of one of them appeared the notice: "Good furmity sold here."

"I always like furmity," said the woman to her husband, "and so does Elizabeth-Jane – and so will you. It's good for you after a long, hard day."

"I've never tasted it," said the man, but they entered the furmity tent right away.

A rather numerous company appeared within, seated at the long narrow table that ran down the tent on each side. At the upper end stood a stove containing a good fire. An old woman of about fifty slowly stirred a pot. The dull scrape of a large spoon sounded throughout the tent as she stirred the mixture of corn, milk, and so on that composed the ancient stuff she dealt in.

The young man and woman ordered a basin each of the mixture, steaming hot, and sat down to eat it. But the man was watching the old woman from the corner of his eye, and saw the game she played. He raised an eyebrow, and passed up his basin in reply to her nod.

She took a bottle from under the table, secretly measured out a quantity of strong drink, and poured it into the man's furmity. Just as secretly, the man sent back money in payment. Now he found the mixture much more to his satisfaction. He finished his basin and called for another, signalling for an even stronger mixture.

His wife sadly noticed the results in his manner, and more than once she said to him, "Michael, how about a place to stay the night? We may not find one if we don't go soon."

But he turned a deaf ear, and talked loud to the company. At the end of the third basin he was argumentative, and after the fourth, quarrelsome.

"I married at eighteen," he informed the company, "like the fool that I was. I haven't more than fifteen shillings in the world, and yet I'd challenge England to beat me in the grain business. If I was a free man again I'd be worth a thousand pounds. When men have wives and don't want 'em, why shouldn't they get rid of 'em

7

– like selling horses? Why shouldn't they sell 'em to men that are in need of such articles?

"By God, I'd sell mine this minute if anybody would buy her! This is your chance – I am open to offers for this jewel among women."

The wife turned to him and whispered, "Michael, you have talked this nonsense in public places before. A joke is a joke, but you may make it once too often."

"I meant it," he said. "All I want is a buyer."

The man went on drinking stronger and stronger basins of furmity, and a quarter of an hour later he came back to the same subject.

"I am waiting to know about this offer of mine. This woman is no good to me. Who'll have her?"

Anxiously the woman whispered, "Come, it's getting dark. If you don't come along, I shall go without you."

She waited, yet he did not move.

"Mike, Mike," she said, "this is getting serious."

"Will any one among you buy my goods?" said the man.

"I wish somebody would," she said firmly. "Her present owner is not at all to her liking!"

"So we are agreed about that," said he. "Gentlemen – you hear? 'Tis an agreement to part. She'll take the girl if she wants to, and go her ways. I'll take my tools and go my ways. Now then, stand up, Susan, and show yourself."

The woman did stand up.

"Now, who'll be the salesman?" said the husband.

8

"I will," answered a short man with a nose like a copper knob, and a damp voice. "Who'll make an offer for this lady?"

"Five shillings," said someone, and there was a laugh.

"Serious offers only," said the husband. "Who'll say a pound?"

Nobody answered.

"Set the price higher," said the man.

"Two pounds," said the salesman, and no one replied.

"Very well," said the husband, "if they don't take her for that, they'll have to give more. Now, salesman, add another."

"Three pounds," said the man with the damp voice.

"Still no offers?" said the husband. "Good Lord, she's cost me fifty times the money. Go on."

"Four pounds!" cried the salesman.

"I'll tell you what – I won't sell her for less than five," said the husband, bringing his hand down so hard that the basins danced. "I'll sell her for five pounds to any man that will treat her well. And he shall have her for ever, and never hear from me. Susan, you agree?"

She nodded her head without expression.

"Five pounds," said the salesman, "or there's no sale. Does anybody give it? The last time. Yes or no?"

"Yes," said a loud voice from the doorway. All eyes were turned. In the door of the tent stood a sailor. A dead silence followed his words.

"Saying is one thing," said the husband, "and

paying is another. Where's the money?"

The sailor unfolded Bank-of-England notes for five pounds, and threw them down upon the tablecloth. With the appearance of real cash, the fun and humour departed from the scene.

"Now," said the woman, in a low, dry voice, "before you go further, Michael, listen to me. If you touch that money, I and this girl go with the man. It is a joke no longer."

"A joke? Of course it's not a joke," shouted the husband. "I take the money – the sailor takes you. That's plain enough."

"It's on the understanding that the young woman is willing," said the sailor softly. "I wouldn't hurt her feelings."

"Of course she's willing," said her husband, "so long as she can have the child. She said so only the other day."

"Do you swear to that?" the sailor asked her.

"I do," she said.

"Very well, the bargain's complete," said the husband.

The sailor looked at the woman and smiled.

"Come along," he said kindly. "The little one too – the more the better!"

She took up the child and followed the sailor to the door. Then she turned, pulled off her wedding-ring, and threw it across the tent in her husband's face. Then, seizing the sailor's arm, she went out of the tent, sobbing bitterly.

A solid look of concern, almost surprise, filled the husband's face, and some of the guests laughed. "Is she gone?" he said.

11

"She's gone, clean enough," said some of the villagers near the door.

He walked unsteadily to the entrance, and stood looking into the dusk. Outside the fair, in the valleys and woods, all was quiet. The sun had recently set, and the west heaven was hung with rosy cloud.

"Where does the sailor live?" said a voice.

"God knows that," replied a man. "He's without doubt a stranger here."

"I'll not go after her," said the husband. "Let her go!"

It was getting late, and the customers soon thinned away from the tent. The man stretched his elbows forward on the table, leant his face upon his arms, and was soon asleep.

The furmity woman put out the last candle, closed the tent door, and drove away.

2

A big blue fly flew round and round in the morning sunlight inside the tent. When the man woke, he looked about – at the long tables, his basket of tools, the stove where the furmity had boiled, the empty basins.

On the grassy floor he noticed a little shining object, and picked it up. It was his wife's ring. A confused picture of the events came back to him, and he pushed his hand into his breast pocket. Dry, papery whispers told him of the sailor's bank-notes. He knew now that his faint memories were not dreams.

He shouldered his tool basket, and went out into the freshness of the September morning. The newly risen sun had not yet dried the damp grass. All the showmen who had remained lay within their carts and tents, or were wrapped in horse-cloths under them, and were silent and still as death.

A little dog barked and quickly lay down again – he was the only witness of the man's exit from Weydon Fair-field. A kilometre away from the field, he leant against a gate.

"She knows I am not in my senses when I say things like that!" he said out loud. "Well, I must walk about till I find her."

Five or six kilometres on, he reached a church and went inside. Dropping his head upon the holy book, he said aloud, "I, Michael Henchard, on this morning of the 16th of September, do swear before God: I will avoid all strong drink for twenty-one years to come – being a year for every year that I have lived. This I swear upon the book before me. May I be struck blind and helpless if I break this promise!"

He kissed the book, and then started on the search for his wife and child. He walked day after day, and examined and inquired. He spent all of the sailor's money on the search, but without any success.

Weeks became months. By this time he arrived at a seaport, where he heard that persons of the right description had sailed from the country a little time before. Then he said he would search no longer.

Next day he journeyed south-westwards, and did not pause till he reached the town of Caster-bridge.

3

The highroad into the village of Weydon-Priors was again carpeted with dust. And where three of the Henchard family had once walked along, two of that family walked now. But it was obvious that a long procession of years had passed by.

The wife of Henchard had lost much of the roundness of her face, her skin had lost its youth, and her hair was thinner. She was dressed in widow's black.

Her companion, also in black, was a well-formed young woman of about eighteen. One look was enough to show you that this was Susan Henchard's grown-up daughter. In the girl's right hand was an old-fashioned basket, and her mother carried her things tied up in a blue cloth.

As before, they made their way to the fair. Here there was more machinery, but fewer places for horses and sheep.

"Why do we waste our time coming here?" said the girl.

"It was here I first met with Newson – on such a day as this."

"First met with father here? And now he's drowned and gone from us!"

As the girl spoke, she took a card from her pocket and looked at it with a sigh. It was edged with black, and on it were the words, "In affectionate memory of Richard Newson, seaman, who was unfortunately lost at sea, in the month of November 1847, aged 41 years."

"And it was here," continued her mother with less confidence, "that I last saw the relative we are looking for – Mr Michael Henchard."

"What relation is he to us exactly, mother? You've never clearly told me."

"He is.... He was.... a connection by marriage," said her mother carefully.

The mother and daughter made their way through the crowd for some little distance, and then stood still. The girl turned to some coloured prints that were on sale.

"Stay here, Elizabeth-Jane," said her mother.

Susan Henchard had seen a pot hanging over a wood fire. Over the pot leant an old woman. She stirred with a large spoon, and occasionally called in a small, dry voice, "Good furmity sold here!"

It was indeed the same woman as before. Susan Henchard-Newson asked for a pennyworth of the thin stuff, and when she had taken the basin, she said cautiously, "Can you call to mind the sale of a wife by her husband in your tent, eighteen years ago today?"

The old woman thought a while and half-shook her head. "A selling? I.... I remember something of the sort – a man in a brown jacket, with a basket of tools. The only reason I remember him is this – he came back here to the next year's fair. If a woman ever asked for him he said, I should say he'd gone to.... where was it?.... Casterbridge? – yes, to Casterbridge."

Susan thanked the woman and went back to Elizabeth-Jane.

"I have learned what I wanted," said the mother quietly. "The last time our relative visited this fair, he was living at Casterbridge. It's a long, long way from here, and it was many years ago that he said it. But there I think we will go."

4

It was at evenfall of a Friday, in late September, when mother and daughter reached the place they searched for. Sometimes they had travelled on foot, sometimes on farmers' carts. And now their steps had brought them to a spot where the town band was shaking the windows of Casterbridge with its brassy music.

The building before whose doors the players had set up their music-stands was the chief hotel in Casterbridge – the King's Arms. From the large open window came the chatter of voices and the ring of glass. The whole of the room could be seen from the street, and a knot of townsfolk had gathered to watch.

"What's going on tonight?" asked the girl.

"Well, you must be a stranger, sure," said an old man. " 'Tis a great public dinner for the leading folk of the town – that's Mr Henchard, the Mayor, at the head of the table."

"Henchard!" said Elizabeth-Jane, surprised.

Susan Henchard stepped up to her daughter's side and looked into the hotel dining-room. Her husband – in law at least – sat before them, straighter, thought-marked. In a word, older. He was dressed in an old-fashioned evening suit, an expensive shirt showing on his broad breast, and a heavy gold chain. Three glasses stood at his right hand, but to his wife's surprise, the two for wine were empty, while the third was full of water.

"They don't fill Mr Henchard's wine-glass," Elizabeth-Jane said to the old man at her elbow.

"Ah no. He won't touch strong drink of any kind. Don't you know that? I've heard that he swore never to have it, in bygone times, and he's kept to his promise ever since."

17

"How much longer has he got to suffer from that?" asked a voice.

"Another two years, they say. And I know that if any of his men take a drop too much, he's down upon them as serious as a judge."

"Has he many men, then?" said Elizabeth-Jane.

"Many? He's a powerful man in the country round here. Wherever there's a big dealing in wheat, hay, roots, and such-like, Henchard's got a hand in it. And he'll go into other things too, and that's where he makes his mistake – I've never before tasted such rough bread as was made from Henchard's wheat lately."

The band now started up another tune, the dinner was over, and speeches began. Henchard's voice rose above the rest, but then a new voice arose from the lower end of the table.

"This is all very well, but how about the bad bread?"

At this, some of the people outside echoed, "Hey! How about the bad bread, Mr Mayor?"

The Mayor could not ignore them. "Well," he said, "I admit the wheat turned out badly. But when I bought it, I was cheated as much as the bakers who bought it from me."

"What are you going to do to repay us?" inquired a man who seemed to be a baker or a miller.

Henchard's face darkened. "If anybody will tell me how to turn poor wheat into good wheat, I'll take it back with pleasure. But it can't be done."

Then Henchard sat down.

The group outside the window had been joined by new arrivals. One of these seemed to be a stranger – a young man of very pleasant appearance – who carried in his hand a carpet-bag with a smart flower-pattern. He was healthy-looking and bright-eyed, and Elizabeth-Jane saw how nicely his hair was cut, and the pleasant curve of his cheek, and how clearly-drawn were his eyelids and eyelashes.

When he heard Henchard's closing words, "It can't be done," he smiled immediately. He took out his pocket-book, and wrote down a few words by the light from the window. He tore out the page, folded and addressed it, and edged forward till he reached the door of the hotel. He gave the note to one of the waiters who was leaning against the doorpost.

"Give this to the Mayor at once," he said.

By his speech he seemed to be a Scotsman. The young stranger continued, "Could you tell me of a hotel around here that's well thought of – and that's a little less expensive than this?"

The waiter looked carelessly down the street. "The Three Sailors, below here – they say it's a very good place. But I've never stayed there myself."

The Scotsman thanked him and walked off in the direction of the Three Sailors. The waiter left the door and Elizabeth-Jane saw the note handed to the Mayor in the dining-room. A clock struck nine.

Susan whispered, "We must get a place to lie down in. I have seen.... Mr Henchard. And that's all I wanted to do."

Elizabeth-Jane said, "Let's go where the young man has gone to. He seemed a man of good character. What do you say?"

Her mother agreed, and down the street they went.

5

At the Three Sailors, Elizabeth-Jane and her mother were shown into a small bedroom just under the roof. The building was ancient, and its passages and doors and windows were awkward and dark, and rarely straight. But quantities of clean white sheets had a pleasing effect on the travellers.

Elizabeth went down and fetched their simple supper, and she pushed open the door of their room with the edge of the tray. To her surprise, her mother lifted a finger. The Scotsman's room was next to their own, and the sound of voices now came through the thin wall between.

Her mother whispered, " 'Tis he."

"Who?" said the girl.

"The Mayor."

The two men were indeed talking in the next

room. The Mayor was saying, "First, I should ask, did you write this note?"

"Yes, I did," said the Scotsman.

"My name is Henchard."

"My name is Donald Farfrae, I am in the corn trade. I am on my way to Bristol – and from there to the other side of the water. I want to try my future in the great wheat-growing districts of the West!"

"To America? – Well, well," said Henchard. "I am truly grateful to you for these few words that you wrote."

"It was nothing, sir."

"Well, it has a great importance for me just now. I have great quantities of wheat in store, all of it poor. If this method of yours really works, and makes it good again, it will get me out of a great deal of trouble. But I should like to have it proved."

The young man said, "Just look here a minute, sir. I can show you the method with some that's in my carpet-bag."

There was the sound of a lock and key, and then a discussion about drying and cooling and so many grams and so on.

"I can show you with these few grains," said the young fellow's voice. After a pause, he cried, "There now! Taste that!"

"It's complete! – well – nearly!"

"Quite good enough to eat," said the Scotsman.

"Listen to me," said Henchard. "My business, you know, is in corn and hay. Hay is what I understand best. If you'll accept the job, you shall manage the corn branch of the business entirely, on a good salary."

"It's kind of you. Very kind. But no. No – I cannot!" the young man replied with some discomfort.

"Very well," said Henchard quickly. "Please yourself. But what shall I pay you for this knowledge?"

"Nothing at all, nothing at all. I don't value it at all, and you were in a difficulty."

Henchard paused. "I shan't soon forget this," he said. "And from a stranger! I am bad at science, Farfrae, bad at figures. And you're just the opposite. Can't you stay and be my manager? I'll make the money worth it to you."

"My plans are fixed. I wish I could stay – truly I would like to. But no – it can't be! I want to see the world."

When Elizabeth-Jane opened the window next morning, the soft air brought in the feel of autumn. Countless brown and yellow leaves brushed along the pavement, and slipped through people's doorways with a nervous scratch on the floor.

Mr Henchard – dressed now as a man of business – was walking down the middle of the street when Donald Farfrae came out of the Three Sailors, bag in hand. Henchard looked at the bag as at an enemy.

"You are off, I suppose," said Henchard.

"Yes," said the other. "Maybe I'll walk on till

the coach catches up with me."

"Then shall we walk together to the top of the town?"

They had passed on and out of sight, and Elizabeth-Jane heard no more. The two new friends walked in silence till they reached a footpath where they had to part.

"Well, here's success to you," said Henchard, holding out his right hand. "But before you are gone forever, I'll speak. Once more, will you stay? Come – name your own conditions. I'll agree to 'em willingly without a word of argument. Damn it, Farfrae, I like you well."

The young man's face reddened. "I never expected this – I did not!" he said. "Maybe it's Fate! Should any man go against it? No, I'll not go to America. I'll stay and be your man!"

"Done!" said Henchard.

"Done!" said Farfrae.

6

It was ten o'clock that morning when Elizabeth-Jane made her way through the High Street. It was a busy market day, and a little inquiry was necessary to guide her footsteps.

Henchard's house was one of the best, with a facing of dull red-and-grey old brick. The front door was open, and she went through to the store-yard. Wherever the doors around the yard were open, closely-packed bags of wheat could be seen inside.

Elizabeth found her way to an office, and there, to her surprise, stood the young Scotsman, Mr Farfrae, pouring some grains of wheat from one hand to the other. She said she wanted to see Mr Henchard.

"Ah yes," he said, and waved her through to an inner office. Elizabeth-Jane entered, and stood before the master of the house.

"Now then, what is it, my young woman?" he said quietly.

"Can I speak to you – not on business, sir?" she said.

"Yes – I suppose." He looked at her more thoughtfully.

"I have been sent to tell you, sir, that a distant relative of yours is in town. A relative by marriage – Susan Newson, a sailor's widow. I am to ask whether you wish to see her."

The rich colours of his complexion changed slightly. "Oh – Susan is – still alive?" he asked with difficulty.

"Yes sir."

"Are you her daughter?"

"Yes sir – her only daughter."

"What.... what do you call yourself – your first name?"

"Elizabeth-Jane, sir."

26

"Newson?"

"Elizabeth-Jane Newson."

This at once suggested to Henchard that the girl knew nothing of the business at Weydon Fair. "I am – a good deal interested in your news," he said. "And as this is not a matter of business, suppose we go indoors."

With a surprisingly gentle manner he showed her out of the office and into the house. In the dining-room, he said, "Sit down – Elizabeth-Jane – sit down," with a shake in his voice as he pronounced her name. "Your mother, then, is quite well?"

"She is rather tired, sir, with travelling."

"A sailor's widow – when did he die?"

"Father was lost last spring." Henchard caught his breath at the word 'father'.

"Do you and she come from abroad – America or Australia?" he asked.

"No, we have been in England for some years. I was twelve when we came here from Canada."

"Ah. And where is your mother staying?"

"At the Three Sailors."

"And you are her daughter Elizabeth-Jane," he repeated. He arose and came close to her, then suddenly turned away with a wet eye. "I think," he said, "you shall take a note from me to your mother. I should like to see her.... She is not left very well-off by her dead husband?"

"Not very well," she said.

He sat down at the table and wrote a few lines. Next he took from his pocket-book a five-pound note, which he put in the envelope with the letter.

"Deliver it to her personally please," said Henchard. "Well, I am glad to see you here, Elizabeth-Jane. Very glad. We must have a long talk together – but not just now."

He took her hand before she left, and held it so warmly that she was much affected, and tears rose to her grey eyes. When she was gone, Henchard shut the door, and sat straight and upright in his dining-room, and stared at the opposite wall as if he read history there.

When Elizabeth reached the Three Sailors, her mother did not read the note at once, but asked Elizabeth to describe her meeting with Henchard, and the exact words he used.

Elizabeth's back was turned when her mother opened the letter, it ran thus:

Meet me at eight o'clock this evening if you can, at the Ring on the Budmouth Road. The place is easy to find. I can say no more now. The news has affected me greatly. The girl seems to be in ignorance. Keep her so, till I have seen you.

M.H.

He said nothing about the five pounds, but the amount was full of meaning. It may silently have said that he bought her back again.

The Ring at Casterbridge was the local name for a huge grassy circle outside the town. Here had stood one of the finest Roman open-air theatres in Britain. The dusk of evening was the proper hour at which a true feeling for this historic circle could be received – sad, serious, and rather grand.

Two figures stood talking together in the middle of the great ring. Susan leant against Henchard, who supported her in his arms.

"I don't drink," he said in a low, apologetic voice. "You hear, Susan? – I don't drink now. I haven't since that night." He felt her lower her head to show she understood. "You have heard that I am in a large way of business here – that I am Mayor of the town, and all that."

"Yes," she whispered.

"And Elizabeth-Jane can't be told all. She would hate us both – I couldn't bear it. These things make it necessary to act with great caution. I don't see how you two can return openly to my house as the wife and daughter I once treated so badly."

"We'll go away at once. I only came to see...."

"No, no, Susan. You are not to go – you mistake me!" he said. "I have thought of this plan: that you and Elizabeth take a cottage in the town, as the widow Newson and her daughter – that I meet you, and get to know you, and marry you – and Elizabeth-Jane comes to my house as my new daughter.

"The thing is so natural and easy. It is half-done in thinking of it. This would leave my early shame as a secret between you and me. And I should have the pleasure of seeing my only daughter under my roof, as well as my wife."

"I am quite in your hands, Michael," she said softly.

"Think over the plans for a few hours," said Henchard. "I have to be away for a day or two on

30

business, unfortunately. But during that time you can get a better place to stay – over one of the shops in the High Street. And you can look for a cottage. Look to me for money."

"I like the idea of repeating our marriage," said Mrs Henchard, after a pause. "Now I think I must go back to Elizabeth-Jane, and tell her that our relation Mr Henchard wishes us to stay in the town."

7

When the Mayor reached home, a light was shining from the office window. Henchard entered and found Farfrae still at work on the books.

"You shall do no more tonight," said Henchard, spreading his great hand over the page of figures. "There's time enough tomorrow. Come and have supper with me. Now you shall!"

The two men walked across the garden and into the house.

Henchard said, "Pull your chair round to the fireplace, my dear fellow. It may seem odd that I should wish to speak to you on family matters, at the end of our first day together. But damn it all, I'm a lonely man, Farfrae. I have nobody else to speak to. And why shouldn't I tell it to you?"

Henchard's firm, deep voice began to shake a little as he began: "I've not always been what I am now...." And he told in fullest detail the story of his dealings with the sailor, and the wife he once had. "And now she has come back, and my daughter with her – this very morning," he said. "And what's to be done?"

"Can you not just take her and live with her, and begin again?"

"Ah, Farfrae," said Henchard sadly. "If I do right by Susan, I must do wrong by another innocent woman."

"You don't say that?"

"For many years I have run across to Jersey in the way of business, especially in the potato and root season. Well, one autumn while I was there, I fell quite ill, and a woman took pity on me – a young lady of good family, well educated. She was as lonely as I was, and she was staying at the same place as myself. She nursed me back to health, Farfrae.

"But we were together in the same house, and her feelings were warm, so we became lovers. At last I was well, and came away. But people there had begun to talk, and her good name was soon in ruins. She has told me of her sufferings in her letters.

"I felt I owed her something, and I asked her to marry me. It was all agreed, and she was full of happiness – but now, Susan appears! I must bitterly disappoint one of these women. But my first duty is to Susan – there's no doubt about that."

Donald showed his deep concern at a complication so far beyond his own simple experiences. "They are both in a very sad position, and that's true," he said. "You must write to the young lady, and say plain and honest that she cannot be your wife, as the first has come back. Say that you wish her well, but you cannot see her any more."

"Now will you help me in this, and write down an explanation for me, and give her the news as gently as you can? I'm so bad at letters."

"I will." Farfrae said no more, but looked for pen and paper, and began the letter to the young Jersey woman.

"It has been a great help, Farfrae, to tell some friend of this," said Henchard. "You see now – the Mayor of Casterbridge is not so well in mind as he is in pocket."

The cottage that Michael Henchard hired for his wife Susan was in the western part of the town. As soon as mother and daughter were comfortably settled in, Henchard began to visit them, and stay to tea. His visits became so frequent and so regular that soon the affair became whispered and then openly discussed in Casterbridge.

Then one afternoon when the daughter was not indoors, Henchard said drily, "This is a very good opportunity for me to ask you to name the happy day, Susan."

Susan Henchard entered a carriage for the first time in her life when it came to her door on the wedding-day. She was so pale that the boys called her 'The Ghost', and no one could understand why Henchard had chosen such a poor, weak woman.

When the pair came out of the church, Christopher Coney said to the woman behind him, "Never before did I see a man wait so long for so little."

The plain little carriage drove off into the fog, and the crowd went their ways.

Michael Henchard was as kind to his wife as a man and a Mayor could possibly be. The house was large, the ceilings were high, and the two soft-footed women hardly made any noticeable addition to the house.

The quiet, easy life was the beginning of a great change in Elizabeth. She found she could have nice personal possessions whenever she wanted. With peace of mind came development, and with development came beauty.

As the winter and spring passed by, her thin face and figure filled out in rounder and softer curves. The lines on her young forehead went away, and good health blossomed in her cheeks.

Meanwhile Henchard's great corn and hay trade profited as never before under the management of Donald Farfrae. Letters and account-books took the place of "I'll do it" and "You shall have it".

8

One day someone in Durnover wanted an opinion on the value of their hay, and sent a messenger. The messenger, who was a child, met Henchard in the yard.

"Very well," said Henchard, "I'll come."

"But please will Mr Farfrae come?" said the child.

"I am going that way. Why Mr Farfrae? Why do people always want Mr Farfrae?"

"I suppose.... because they like him – that's what they say."

"Oh – I see – that's what they say, eh? They like him because he's cleverer than Mr Henchard, and because he knows more – eh?"

"Yes, that's just it, sir. Some of it."

"Oh? There's more? What else? Come, here's sixpence for you."

"They say Mr Farfrae's better-tempered, and he's the one that's really in charge. And some of the women say, 'I wish he was master instead of Henchard.' "

"They'll talk any nonsense," Henchard replied with a heavy heart. "Well, you can go now. And *I* am coming to value the hay, d'you hear? I."

The boy departed. When Henchard left for Durnover, he overtook Farfrae, and they walked together.

"By the way," said Donald, "the people in Durnover want their hay valued."

"Yes, I'm going there."

"I'll go with you."

Henchard did not reply.

"You're not your usual self today?" Donald inquired.

"I am very well," said Henchard.

"But surely you're a bit downhearted?"

Henchard looked mostly on the ground. "I have been hearing things that annoyed me," he said. "That was what made me unfriendly in my manner. But look here, Farfrae, you can do it better than I can. They asked for you too. I have to be at a meeting at eleven o'clock, and it's nearly that now."

So they parted in renewed friendship. Donald did not ask Henchard for meanings that were not very plain to him. And Henchard's face was untroubled again.

But whenever he thought of Farfrae now, he regretted that he had told the young man his whole heart, and the secrets of his life.

Henchard's manner towards Farfrae became gradually more formal. He was polite – too polite. He never again put his arm upon the young man's shoulder. He no longer went to Farfrae's rooms and shouted, "Hoy, Farfrae, boy, come and have some dinner with us! Don't sit here all by yourself!"

Thus their lives rolled on till a day of public holiday. Farfrae said he was thinking of setting up an entertainment, and asked Henchard about the loan of some hay-cloths.

"Have as many cloths as you like," Henchard replied.

When his manager had gone about the business, the idea began to take fire in Henchard's mind. As Mayor, he too ought to organize some amusements. So Henchard began his preparations for a real grand affair, and unlike Farfrae's, his would be free. ("Charge for admission? Just like a Scotsman! Who is going to pay to go in?")

Henchard chose for his event a field that sloped down to the river, and he advertised about the town in long pink posters. Under his own eye an army of men prepared games of all sorts.

They put up slippery posts for climbing, with smoked hams and local cheeses at the top. They placed wooden bars in rows for jumping over. They laid a smooth post across the river, with a live pig tied at the other end – to become the property of the first man who could walk over and get it. They provided donkeys for racing, and a stage for boxing. And Henchard provided a huge tea, which everyone was invited to take without payment.

The morning came, and at twelve o'clock the rain began to fall, small and steady. In an hour, the shower had become an attack on earth by the

floods of heaven. Towards six, the storm cleared, and a dry wind shook the water from the grass. The band was called out from its shelter, and the tables were carried away to leave space for dancing.

"But where are the folk?" said Henchard, after a half hour in which only two men and a woman had stood up to dance.

"They're all at Farfrae's affair in the West Walk," answered one of the men.

Henchard walked away thoughtfully. He soon found that most people were walking towards the sound of a stringed band, and he made his way there himself. He came to a huge tent that had been cleverly constructed without posts or ropes. The cloths had been hung from the branches of an avenue of trees, and the end towards the wind was enclosed.

A lively dance of some sort was in progress, and in the middle of all was Farfrae, dressed as a wild Scots Highlander, throwing himself about and spinning to the tune. Henchard noticed the keen admiration in the women's faces. He walked and waited till his wife was ready to go home.

When he went back to the tent, Farfrae was footing a country dance with Elizabeth-Jane – the only one she knew. The leaping tune had tempted her into it, and Farfrae had softened his movements to suit her. It was soon over, and the girl looked at Henchard for approval, but he did not give it.

One of the townsmen came up and said, "You see, Mr Henchard? You should have had your sports in a sheltered place like this. But you didn't think of it, you see, and he did. And that's where he's beat you."

"No," said Henchard. "He won't do that, because he's shortly going to leave me." He looked towards Donald. "Mr Farfrae's time as my manager is coming to an end – isn't it, Farfrae?"

It was quickly known in Casterbridge that Farfrae and Henchard had decided to part. Elizabeth-Jane's anxiety reached a depth that disturbed her, and she could no longer hide from herself the cause.

But then the news reached her that Farfrae was not going to leave the place. A man had sold his business to him, and Farfrae was now about to start up in the corn and hay trade for himself. Henchard was hurt, and then angry, when he heard the news at a meeting in the Town Hall. When he came home, he called Elizabeth-Jane.

"That man Farfrae – have you made him any foolish promise?"

"No, I have promised him nothing."

"Good. I especially wish you not to see him again."

"Very well, sir, if you wish it."

"I do. He's an enemy to our house."

When she had gone, he sat down and wrote to Farfrae:

Sir, — I request that from this moment on, you and my daughter be strangers to each other. She has promised to welcome no more interest from you. I trust, therefore, that you will not attempt to force any upon her.

M. HENCHARD

Almost every Saturday the two men met in the market-place. Donald was always ready to say a few friendly words, but the Mayor stared stormfully past him.

If at breakfast or dinner, Elizabeth-Jane's mother accidentally mentioned Farfrae's name, her husband would say, "What – are you too my enemy?"

9

One day Elizabeth-Jane's mother was ill, and Henchard sent at once for the richest, busiest doctor (whom he supposed to be the best). Elizabeth stayed up with her mother all night, and did not appear at breakfast.

Henchard sat down at table alone that morning, and was surprised to see a letter for him from Jersey. It was in a writing he knew too well, and had not expected to see again. The writer said she well understood that his remarriage was necessary. She went on:

I see that there can be no future relationship between us. And I am sure you will see, Michael, that my future happiness depends on one thing — that our past connection be kept secret. I know you will not speak of it, and I trust you not to write of it. There is one more protection I wish to mention — may I ask you to return to me any of my writings in your possession (especially the letters I wrote during those first wild months). I am now on my way to Bristol to see my only relative. I shall return through Casterbridge. Can you meet me with the letters? I shall be in the coach which changes horses at the Antelope Hotel at half-past five on Wednesday evening. I remain still, yours ever,

LUCETTA

Henchard tied up Lucetta's letters into a parcel, and on the appointed day he went at dusk and stood opposite the coach-office. The evening was cold, and the coach was late. Henchard crossed over to it while the horses were being changed, but there was no Lucetta inside or out. He gave the matter up and went home.

Meanwhile Mrs Henchard was weakening. At a time when she was alone, she wrote upon a sheet of paper, folded and stuck it down, then locked it in her desk. She had addressed it in these words: *Mr Michael Henchard. Not to be opened till Elizabeth-Jane's wedding-day.*

Some little time later, Farfrae was passing Henchard's house on a Sunday morning, when he noticed that the curtains were all closed. He rang the bell softly, and was informed that Mrs Henchard had died only an hour before.

At the town pump, a few of the older folk had gathered for water. As Farfrae passed, they were talking of Mrs Henchard.

"Well, poor heart, she's beyond all help now," said Mother Cuxsom. "And all her shining keys will be taken from her, and her cupboards will be opened. Everyone will see what she did not wish seen. And her wishes will all be as nothing!"

Henchard and Elizabeth sat talking by the fire. It was three weeks after the burial. The candles were not lighted, and a restless flame, dancing on a coal, called soft shapes from the shady walls.

"Elizabeth," said Henchard, "was Newson a kind father?"

"Yes sir. Very."

"Suppose I had been your father," he said. "Would you have cared for me as much as you cared for Newson?"

"I can't think of it," she said quickly. "I can't think of any other as my father, except my father."

Henchard walked up and down, and then he came and stood behind her chair, looking down upon the top of her head. He had lost his wife – he had lost his friend Farfrae – he had lost his daughter. Only one of them could be recalled, and that was the girl.

"What did your mother tell you about me – my history?" he asked.

"That you were related by marriage."

"She should have told you more! Then my duty would not be such a hard one.... But, it is I who am your father, and not Richard Newson."

The back of Elizabeth's head remained still, and her shoulders did not show even the movements of her breathing.

Henchard went on, "Your mother and I were man and wife when you were young. What you saw was our second marriage. Each had thought the other was dead – and – Newson became her husband."

This was the nearest approach that Henchard could make to the full truth.

"Don't cry – don't cry," he said with sudden feeling. "I can't bear it. I won't bear it. I am your father – why should you cry? Am I so hateful to you Elizabeth-Jane?" he cried, taking her hand, "I'll be kinder to you than *he* was! I'll do anything, if you'll only look upon me as your father."

She tried to stand up and face him trustfully, but she could not. She was troubled at his presence.

"I don't want you to come to me all of a sudden," he said. "No Elizabeth, I don't. I'll go away and not see you till tomorrow, or whenever you like. And then I'll show you papers to prove my words. There, I'm gone, and I won't disturb you any more. Goodnight, my Elizabeth-Jane!"

He went out at the door softly, and she remained in silence and sobbed – not for her mother now, but for the lovable sailor Richard Newson, to whom she seemed to be doing a wrong.

Henchard in the meantime had gone upstairs. Among his papers he found the letter from his wife: *Not to be opened till Elizabeth-Jane's wedding-day.* There was no envelope: the sheet was not properly stuck down, and had fallen open. Without curiosity he allowed his eyes to run along the lines of handwriting:

My dear Michael — for the good of all three of us, I have kept a secret from you till now. I shall be in my grave when you read this, and Elizabeth-Jane will have a home. I can hardly write it, Michael, but here it is. Elizabeth-Jane is not your Elizabeth-Jane — the child who was in my arms when you sold me. No — she died three months after that, and this living one is my other husband's. I gave her the same name, and she filled up the ache that I felt at the other's loss. Michael, I am dying, and I might have kept my secret, but I could not. Forgive me if you can, as I forgive you.

SUSAN HENCHARD

Her husband looked at the paper as if it was glass, through which he saw into the far distance.

The morning came after a night of suffering and unrest. The moment he came into the breakfast-room, Elizabeth advanced to him and took him by the arm.

"I have thought and thought all night of it," she said. "And I am going to look upon you as the father you are, and I am not going to call you Mr Henchard any more. Now, father, breakfast is ready!" she said cheerfully.

Henchard bent and kissed her cheek. For weeks he had looked forward to this moment with deep pleasure. But now the fruit of the whole plan had become dust and ashes.

10

Of all the puzzles that ever confused a girl, there can be few like Henchard's sudden change of behaviour towards Elizabeth. From the next morning onwards, his manner was formal as she had never seen it before. His two years as Mayor were coming to an end, and the consciousness of it helped to sour him. The coldness soon broke out into open complaint.

One serious failing of Elizabeth's was her occasional pretty use of country words.

"Good God!" he cried sharply. "Are you only fit to carry buckets to the pigs, that you use such words as those?"

She reddened with shame and sadness. She would go to the kitchen instead of ringing the bell, "so as not to make Phoebe come up twice." She went down on her knees to clear up, when the cat overturned the coals. And she always thanked the maid-servant for everything, till one day Henchard broke out with "Good God, will you stop thanking that girl as if she was goddess-born! Don't I pay her a dozen pounds a year to do things for you?"

Henchard showed a positive distaste for the presence of this girl who was not his own. He mostly dined with the farmers at one of the two chief hotels, leaving her all alone. He now regretted his note to Farfrae, forbidding him to meet Elizabeth. If Farfrae would take her, Henchard would be rid of her completely.

At last he wrote Farfrae a second note:

Sir, — I have been reconsidering the matter of yourself and Elizabeth-Jane. I do not wish to interfere between the two of you, if you care for her. I therefore take back my objection — except that the business must not take place in my house.

Yours, M. HENCHARD

Winter had almost come, and Elizabeth-Jane seized on one of the last days of pale autumn sunshine to visit the spot where her mother lay buried. She reached the churchyard at about half-past ten in the morning, but someone was there before her.

A single dark figure was reading the words on Mrs Henchard's gravestone. It was a lady, beautifully dressed, and Elizabeth felt all her own freshness and prettiness stolen away by this stranger. This was clearly no country woman from Casterbridge.

When Elizabeth at last stood before the grave in some confusion, the lady said, "I guess how it is with you." She waved her hand towards the gravestone. "That was your mother."

"Yes," said Elizabeth, "my only friend."

"But your father, Mr Henchard, is he living?"

"Yes, he is living," said Elizabeth-Jane.

"Is he not kind to you?"

"I have no wish to complain of him."

"There has been a disagreement?"

"A little. It is all my fault, I dare say. And my faults are owing to my history."

"What is your history?"

"It is not very attractive. And yet I can tell it if you really want to know."

The lady replied that she did want to know, and Elizabeth-Jane told her the story of her life as she knew it.

"I don't know how to return," she ended. "I think of going away. But what can I do?"

"Perhaps it will be better soon," said her friend gently. "Now what do you think of this: I shall soon want somebody to live in my house – partly as housekeeper, partly as companion. Would you like to come to me? But perhaps...."

"Oh yes," cried Elizabeth with tears in her eyes. "I would indeed. But where do you live?"

"In Casterbridge – after twelve o'clock tomorrow. My house is getting ready. It is the one they call High-Place Hall – the old stone one looking down on to the market-place. Now will you think over my offer? My name is Miss Templeman. Come and see me when you know your mind."

Henchard was not a little amazed at receiving a letter in Lucetta's well-known handwriting:

HIGH-PLACE HALL. MY DEAR MR HENCHARD,—

48

Don't be surprised. It is for your own good as well as mine, as I hope, that I have come to live in Caster-bridge. I am sorry I was delayed the other day, and unable to keep my appointment with you. I am here because I have heard of the death of your wife, poor woman. I thought I now ought to ask you to carry out your promise to me. But I did not know your position, or what had happened since our separation. So I decided to settle myself here before getting a message to you. I shall be able to see you in a day or two. Till then, farewell.

Yours, *LUCETTA*

Henchard thought of himself as a childless man, and he badly needed to fill the emptiness in his heart. He thought of Lucetta with interest, indeed with warmth. He showed no more anger towards Elizabeth: he showed something worse – a complete lack of interest.

"Father, have you any objection to my going away?" she asked.

"Going away! No – none at all. Where are you going?"

"I have a chance of a place in a good house. I will have the advantages of study, and I can learn perhaps to become a lady."

"Then make the best of it, in heaven's name."

"I shall not be far away, and if you want me badly I can soon come back again."

He nodded slightly. "What will be your address? Or am I not to know?"

"Oh yes – certainly. It is only in the town – High-Place Hall."

"Where?" said Henchard, his face still.

She repeated the words. He neither moved nor

spoke, and she turned and left him.

11

Lucetta was a keen letter-writer, and Elizabeth had hardly gone away when another note came to the Mayor's house from High-Place Hall:

I am now settled in here. You are probably aware of my arrangement with your daughter, and you have doubtless laughed at my little joke. Do you see, Michael, why I have done it? It gives you an excuse for coming here, as if to visit her. In this way you can call at my house naturally.

Yours always, LUCETTA

The excitement that crept into Henchard's empty heart was most pleasurable. He sat over his dining-table long and dreamily. Lucetta was clearly in a willing mood for marriage. "The artful little woman!" he said with a smile.

Next morning Lucetta dressed herself for Mr Henchard, and restlessly awaited his call before mid-day. As he did not come, she waited through the afternoon, but still he did not arrive. More days came, but not the visitor. He must have been too busy, she thought.

Tuesday was the day of the fair. At breakfast

Lucetta said to Elizabeth-Jane quite coolly, "I imagine your father may call to see you today."

Elizabeth shook her head. "He won't come."

"Why?"

"His mood is against me."

"You have quarrelled more deeply than I know of."

"Yes."

"Then where you are is – of all places – the one that he will avoid?"

Elizabeth nodded sadly. Lucetta burst into wild sobs. Here was disaster – her neat plan lay in ruins.

"Oh, my dear Miss Templeman – what's the matter?" cried her companion.

"I – I – " But she could not finish. If Henchard had such a rooted dislike for the girl, Lucetta would have to get rid of her. An idea suggested itself.

"Miss Henchard – will you do something for me, as soon as breakfast is over? Will you go and order...." Here she listed several things to be bought from various shops. They would take up Elizabeth's time for the next hour or two at least.

Elizabeth put on her things and left. "I wonder why she wants to get rid of me today?" she thought sorrowfully as she went out.

Within ten minutes one of Lucetta's servants was sent to Henchard with a note:

DEAR MICHAEL,—Do please call and see me. I am sadly disappointed that you have not come before. I have sent your daughter away for the morning. Say that you have come on business — I shall be quite alone.

LUCETTA

She arranged herself prettily in a chair, so that the light fell over her head. There she remained till a man's step was heard on the stairs. At that moment Lucetta ran and hid herself behind one of the window-curtains in sudden shyness. She heard the servant show the visitor into the room and shut the door behind him. Lucetta threw back the curtain with a nervous greeting.

The man before her was not Henchard.

Lucetta's visitor was years younger than the Mayor of Casterbridge: fair, fresh, and handsome.

Lucetta reddened, and said with a curious mixture of anxiety and laughter, "Oh, I've made a mistake!"

"But I'm very sorry," he said, "I came and inquired for Miss Henchard, and they showed me up here. Have I come to the wrong house, madam?" said Mr Farfrae in some confusion.

"Oh, no, sir – you must come and sit down, now that you are here," replied Lucetta kindly. "Miss Henchard will be here in a moment."

Now this was not true, but something about the young man was attractive to Lucetta. The fair outside the windows was now storming thick and loud. "The fair today seems a large one," she said.

"Do you look out often?"

"Yes – very often."

"Maybe you are very lonely, ma'am."

"Nobody knows how lonely. I came to Casterbridge, thinking I should like to live here. But I wonder if I shall."

"It's better to stay at home, and that's true. I am from Edinburgh. But a man must live where his money is made. It is a pity. Yet I've done very well this year. You see that man with the dull brown coat? I bought a lot from him in the autumn, when the wheat prices were down. Then when the prices rose a little, I sold off all I had!

"It brought only a small profit. But the farmers kept their wheat, expecting higher figures. I bought up their corn when the markets were low. Then I sold it a few weeks after, when by chance it went down again!

"I was content with small profits, frequently repeated, and I soon made five hundred pounds – while others kept theirs in hand, and made nothing at all!"

Then his eye met the lady's. "Ay, now, I'm wearying you," he said.

"No indeed," she said quickly. "You are most interesting."

"I don't know how to talk to ladies, and that's the truth," said Donald with regret. "I try to be polite to people – no more!"

Outside, in the street, below the open windows, two farmers met and shook hands.

"Have you seen young Mr Farfrae this morning?" asked one.

Hearing them, Lucetta said, "Now you must go, or you will lose a customer."

"Now, Miss Templeman, you will make me angry," he cried.

"Then suppose you don't go, but stay a little longer?"

"I like staying, but I fear I must go. I'll come another time – if I may, ma'am?"

"Certainly," she said. "But now the market calls you to be gone."

"Market – business! I wish there was no business in the world. I have never wished such things before," said the Scotsman, with a simple, shamed, apologetic look. "It is only since coming here and seeing you!"

"Thank you for staying."

Farfrae was shown out, and it entirely escaped his mind that he had called to see Elizabeth.

Three minutes later heavy knocking sounded through the house, and the maid came up.

"The Mayor," she said.

Lucetta was looking dreamily through her fingers. "Tell him I have a headache. I won't delay him today."

12

Day after day, Lucetta's silence proved to Henchard that she was not going to come to him. So he gave in and called upon her again when Elizabeth-Jane was absent.

"It is very good of you to call," she said.

"But of course I have called, Lucetta," he said. "What does that nonsense mean? I have come to say that I am ready to give you my name in marriage – to say that you can fix the day or month whenever in your opinion it would be proper. You know more of these things than I do."

"It is full early yet," she said, avoiding his eyes.

"Yes, yes, I suppose it is. Still, I come to you with an honest offer for silencing your enemies in Jersey, and you ought to be thankful."

"How can you speak to me like that!" she answered quickly. "My only crime was to show a foolish girl's love for you – more than was proper."

"And I therefore think you ought to accept me – for your own good name's sake."

"For the present, let things be," she said. "Treat me as a friend, and I'll treat you as one."

"So that's the way the wind blows, is it?" he said.

A yellow flood of sunlight filled the room for a few moments. It was produced by the passing of a load of hay in the street below, in a cart marked with the name FARFRAE. Beside it rode Farfrae himself on horseback. Henchard did not notice the changed look on Lucetta's face.

As he went out through the door, he said, "You came to live in Casterbridge entirely because of me. Yet now that you're here, you have nothing to say to my offer!"

From this time, both men hardly seemed to see Elizabeth-Jane. When Lucetta hurt her finger, they were as deeply concerned as if she was dying: when Elizabeth-Jane was seriously sick or in danger, they offered a polite word of sympathy at the news, and forgot all about it immediately.

She knew now that she had lost Donald Farfrae for ever. And she wondered what unwished-for thing heaven might send her in place of him.

13

In a lonely place a few kilometres from the town, there lived a man with a curious kind of fame: that he could tell you the future. The way to his house was winding and muddy.

One evening when the rain on the leaves sounded like gunshots, a well-wrapped figure had travelled on foot towards the wood that sheltered the man's cottage. The tall traveller held a hand-kerchief to his face, as if he was suffering from toothache.

"No I won't come in," he said.

"As you wish," said the man at the door, with a candle in his hand.

"I hear that you can – do things of a sort?"

"Maybe so, Mr Henchard," said the other.

"Ah – why do you call me that?" said the other with a jump of surprise.

"Because it's your name. I had a feeling you'd

come if I waited for you. I've laid two supper-plates."

After a moment's silence, Henchard said, "Can you tell the weather that's to come?"

"After work and time."

"Then take this coin," said Henchard. "Now – what's the harvest weather to be like? When can I know?"

"I've worked it out already, and you can know at once." (The fact was that five farmers had already been there for the same information, from different parts of the country.) "By the sun, moon, and stars, by the clouds, the winds, the trees and grass, the candle-flame and birds of the sky, also by the cat's eyes...."

"Yes?"

".... the last two weeks of August will be –rain and storm."

"You are not certain of course?"

"As certain as one can be in a world where all's unsure."

The next Saturday, Henchard bought so much grain that there was quite a talk among his neighbours. He bought more grain on the next day, and on all possible days.

When his buildings were full to bursting, the wind came around as if tired of the south-west. The weather changed. The sky, which had been like dull tin for weeks, brightened to a shade of yellow. An excellent harvest was almost a certainty, and prices rushed down. Henchard had risked his money on bad weather, and seemed to have lost. He had to sell off, at a low price, corn he had bought only a few weeks before. He lost heavily. Soon much of Henchard's property was the possession of his bankers.

As prices were low, Farfrae was buying. There were three days of excellent weather, and then – on the day when the harvesting began – there was water in the air. It rubbed people's cheeks like a wet cloth as they walked. There was a high, warm wind, and raindrops began to star the windows. If Henchard had only waited longer....

Meanwhile Donald Farfrae's wealth increased.

"He'll soon be Mayor," said Henchard.

The harvest was delayed by the weather, so whenever a fine day came along, nearly the whole town went into the fields to try and save the damaged crops. Because of the shortening of the days, the harvesters worked by moonlight.

Their shouts and laughter reached Henchard in the market square, and he made his way towards them. As he reached a shaded avenue, two others were coming towards him. A meeting promised to be awkward, so he stepped into the shadows and sat down.

"Say what you like," Lucetta was saying gaily.

"Well then," replied Farfrae in the unmistakable voice of the lover, "with all your wealth and beauty, you are sure to have lots of admirers. Will you be happy enough with only one?"

"And that one is yourself?" said she, laughing.

"Very well, sir. You know, Donald, that I love nobody else. But I would wish to have my own way in some things."

"In everything."

They went on into the fields, and Lucetta left Farfrae when they were getting near to the work-people. Henchard hurried back to Lucetta's house. He did not knock, but went straight up to her sitting-room. In a few minutes he heard the whisper of her dress in the hall, and the soft closing of a door. In a moment she appeared. As soon as she saw him, she gave out a little cry, almost of terror.

"I have a little matter to remind you of, Lucetta, which you seem to forget."

She sank into a chair and turned pale. "I don't want to hear it – I don't want to hear it!" she said through her hands.

"Why did you come here to Casterbridge?"

"I thought I ought to marry you, since you were free, even though I – did not like you so well."

"And why don't you think so now?"

She was silent.

"The man you are thinking of is not better than I am," he said.

"If you were as good as he is, you would leave me!" she cried.

"You can't in honour refuse me," said Henchard. "If you do not promise me this very night to be my wife – before a witness – I'll make public our true relationship – in fairness to other men!"

A look of weariness settled upon her. Henchard saw its bitterness. Without another word she rang

the bell, and asked for Elizabeth-Jane. When the girl appeared, she went across to her father dutifully.

"Elizabeth-Jane," said Henchard, taking her hand, "I want you to hear this," and he turned to Lucetta: "Will you or will you not marry me?"

"If you – if you wish it, I must agree!"

"You say yes?"

"I do." When she had given her promise, she fell back into a chair.

"You are a witness," Henchard said to Elizabeth-Jane. "She has agreed to be my wife."

"I have, I have," groaned Lucetta, in a faint voice full of pain. "Michael, please don't argue it any more!"

"I will not," he said. And taking up his hat, he went away.

Elizabeth-Jane continued to kneel by Lucetta. "What is this?" she said. "You called my father 'Michael' as if you knew him well. And how has he got this power over you? Why do you promise to marry him against your will? Ah – you have many secrets from me!"

14

The next morning Henchard went to the Town Hall. Because he had lately been Mayor, he was a magistrate, and took his place in the big chair at the front of the police court.

There was one case only – an old woman in a dirty black hat and ancient clothes. She looked briefly at Henchard and the second magistrate, and Henchard thought she reminded him of somebody or something.

"Well, and what has she been doing?" he said.

"She is accused of being disorderly, sir," whispered the policeman.

"Where did she do that?" said the other magistrate.

"By the church, sir, of all the horrible places in the world. I caught her in the act, sir."

"Stand back then, Stubberd," said Henchard, "and let's hear what you've got to say."

The policeman swore to tell the truth, the whole truth, and nothing but the truth, and the magistrates' clerk lowered his pen into the ink.

Stubberd began – "Hearing an illegal noise at twenty-five minutes past eleven on the night of the fifth of this month...."

"Not so fast, Stubberd," said the clerk.

The policeman waited with his eyes on the pen till the clerk had stopped writing, and said, "Yes."

"I went down the street to the spot, and I saw the accused person at another spot. She was unsteady on her feet, and wandering about in a quite dangerous manner. When I approached her, she became disorderly, and began to use bad language."

"Bad language? What did she say?"

"She said, 'Put away that d---- lamp,' she says."

"That dee lamp?"

"Yes sir. 'D'you hear, old cabbage-head,' she says. 'Put away that dee lamp. I have knocked down fellows that were dee finer-looking than a dee fool like you – dee me,' she says."

Henchard became impatient. "Come – we don't need to hear any more of these dees. If you mean *damn*, then say the word out like a man, Stubberd, or else leave it alone." Henchard turned to the woman. "Now then, have you anything to say?"

"Yes," she replied with an artful look in her eye, and the clerk inked his pen again. "About twenty years ago, I was selling furmity in a tent at Weydon Fair...."

"Twenty years ago!" said the clerk. "Well! That's beginning at the beginning!" But Henchard stared and was silent.

"A man and a woman with a little child came into my tent," the woman continued. "They sat

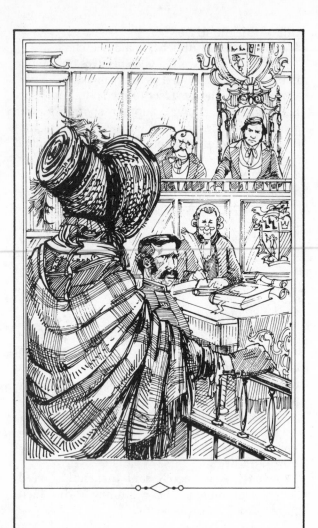

down and had a basin each. I used to put a drop or two of strong drink into my furmity, for them that asked for it.

"I did it for the man, and he had more and more – till at last he quarrelled with his wife and offered to sell her. A sailor came and paid five pounds and led her away. And the man who sold his wife in that fashion? – he is the man sitting there in the great big chair."

She ended by nodding her head at Henchard, and folding her arms. Everybody looked at Henchard. His face seemed strange, as if it had been powdered over with ashes.

"We don't want to hear your life and adventures," said the second magistrate sharply. "You've been asked if you have anything to say about this case."

"It *is* about this case. It proves he's not better than I am. And he has no right to sit there in judgment upon me."

"It's an invented story," said the clerk, "so hold your tongue!"

"No – it is true." The words came from Henchard. "It is as true as I live," he said slowly. "Indeed it does prove that I'm no better than she is! And so that I will not treat her hard for revenge, I'll leave her to you."

The sensation in the court was indescribably great. Henchard left the chair and went out.

"Why are there so many people round the Town Hall today?" said Lucetta to her servant when the case was over. She had risen late and just looked out of her window.

"Oh, please, ma'am, it's all this upset about Mr Henchard. A woman has proved that before he became a gentleman he sold his wife for five pounds at a fair."

A gradual sorrow overspread Lucetta's face as she remembered her promise of the night before. At bottom, then, Henchard was this. What a terrible piece of news for a woman who was about to come into his care.

She told Elizabeth-Jane that she had decided to go away from home to the seaside for a few days – to Port-Bredy: Casterbridge was such an unhappy place. Elizabeth took charge of High-Place Hall till her return.

After two or three days of loneliness and continuous rain, Henchard called at the house. He seemed disappointed to hear of Lucetta's absence. The next day, he called again,

"Is she come now?" he asked.

"Yes. She returned this morning," replied Elizabeth. "She has gone for a walk along the road towards Port-Bredy. She will be home by dusk."

Lucetta was returning from her walk along the Port-Bredy road, and she had reached the beginning of the ranked trees that led into Casterbridge. It was here that she met Henchard, who was now holding her hand within his arm.

"Dear Lucetta, I have been very anxious to see you these two or three days," he said. "Ever since I saw you last! I have thought over the way I got your promise that night. I don't want to cause you pain. Therefore I agree to put off our marriage for a year or two.... In any case, I should take the time to put my business in order.

"You may have heard that I have been unlucky this year. I did what I have never done before – I took a foolish risk, and I lost. That's put me in a difficulty."

"And you would wish me to lend you some money."

"No, no," said Henchard, almost in anger. "I'm not the man to take money from a woman, even though she is almost my own wife. No, Lucetta. What you can do is this: and it would save me. The man that I owe most money to is Grower. If he would not call in his debt for another two weeks, I would be able to survive. And I think he could be persuaded – if you could let him know that we'll be married after two weeks. He knows you have money and to spare."

"But I can't...."

"Now stop, you haven't heard all! We are not really going to marry so soon. But you could go with me to Mr Grower, and make him *believe* we were ready for marriage. We'll ask him to keep it secret – he'll willingly wait then. At the end of two weeks I shall be able to pay him. And I can coolly tell him that all is put off between us for a year or two. Nobody in the town need know how you've helped me."

In the growing dusk, he did not notice the effect of his words upon her.

"If it were anything else," she began with dry lips.

"But it is such a little thing!" he said.

"It is not because I won't – it's because I simply can't," she said with rising anxiety.

"Why? – when I have just freed you from your promise to marry me at once."

"Because – he was a witness!"

"Witness? Of what?"

"If I must tell you...."

"Well! Let's hear what you mean."

"Mr Grower was a witness of my marriage!"

"Marriage?"

"Yes. With Mr Farfrae. Oh, Michael, I am already his wife. We were married this week at Port-Bredy."

For a moment Henchard stood as if he had lost the power of speech. Then at last he said, "Married him? Married *him?* While you were promised to me?"

There were tears in her eyes, and her voice shook. "Don't – don't be cruel! I loved him so much, and I thought you might tell him of our past. Then I learned that you had sold your first wife at a fair, like a horse or cow. How could I keep my promise after hearing that? But I knew I would lose Donald if I did not secure him at once – but you will not tell him of our past now, will you, Michael? It is too late to separate us."

The notes of the church bells were carried through the air to them as she spoke. And now the happy beat of the town band thundered down the street.

"Then this noise is because of your wedding, I suppose," said he.

"Yes. I think Donald has told them, or Mr Grower has. May I leave you now? My husband was delayed at Port-Bredy today, and sent me on a few hours before him."

"Oh, you false woman!" burst from Henchard. "And now I ought to punish you for your wrongs. One word of our past to this new husband of yours, and your precious happiness is blown to atoms!"

"Michael – pity me, and be generous! I'll help you to pay off your debt."

"A debtor of Farfrae's wife – not I! Don't stay with me longer – I shall say something worse. Go home!"

She disappeared under the trees of the south walk as the band came round the corner, sounding out her happiness. Lucetta ran up the back street and reached her own home unseen.

"Oh, you *have* married him!" cried Elizabeth-Jane, jumping up with pleasure as Lucetta came into the room. Her eyes were on the ring on Lucetta's left hand. "When did you do it? Why did you not tell me? How very honourable of you! He did treat my mother badly once, it seems, when he had had too much to drink. But you will rule him entirely, I am sure, with your beauty and wealth. You are the woman he will love, and we shall all three be happy together now!"

"O, my Elizabeth-Jane," cried Lucetta, close to tears. "It is not your father I have married! It is someone else. I was so afraid that certain secrets would be uncovered, and kill his love for me. So I decided to buy a week of happiness at any cost!"

"You – have – married Mr Farfrae!" cried Elizabeth-Jane.

"My husband is downstairs," said Lucetta. "He will live here till a more suitable house is ready for us. And I want you to stay with me just as before. I am sure we shall be happy together."

Lucetta departed to join Donald below. And the immediate decision of Susan Henchard's daughter was to live in that house no more. It was still early evening when she went out and found suitable rooms. They were in the street in which Henchard lived, and almost opposite his door.

15

The words of the furmity woman had spread, and in twenty-four hours all of Casterbridge knew the story of Henchard's madness at Weydon-Priors Fair, long years before. Within one day, he passed over the hilltop of wealth and honour, and began to go down quickly on the other side.

He was unable to pay his debts, and he now stared more at the pavements and less at the house-fronts; more at men's feet, and less into their eyes.

Elizabeth believed in him still, though nobody else did, but she could never meet with him. She wrote to him: he did not reply. She went to his house – the great house where she had lived so happily for a time – but Henchard was there no more.

They told her, "He has gone to live in Jopp's cottage by the mill. He has a couple of rooms there."

But even there Henchard could not be seen.

"Not by his daughter?" said Elizabeth.

"By nobody – at present. That's his order."

Afterwards she passed by the stores of corn and hay that had been the headquarters of Henchard's trade. She stared with amazement at the familiar gateway. Lead-coloured paint had been firmly laid on to cover Henchard's name. Over this, in fresh white, spread the name Farfrae.

From now on, the full bags of corn, tied with shining chains, went hurrying up and down on ropes. Hairy arms appeared from the different doorways, and the grain was pulled in. And scales and steel balances were busy where guesswork had once been the rule.

Elizabeth-Jane was determined to improve her mind. In her small upper room, she studied all the books she could get hold of. From her window she could see Donald and Lucetta speeding in and out of the door of Henchard's old house. She avoided looking that way as much as possible, but it was hardly in human nature to turn her eyes away all the time.

While she was living thus quietly, she heard the news that Henchard had caught cold, and had to keep to his room. She went off to him at once. He was sitting up in bed with a greatcoat round him.

"Go away – go away," he said. "I don't like to see you!"

"But father...."

"I don't like to see you!" he repeated.

But she remained, and made the room more comfortable, and gave orders to the people below, and talked to Henchard. The effect of her help, or perhaps simply of her presence, was a rapid recovery.

He soon was well enough to go out, and now things seemed to wear a new colour in his eyes. He thought more and more of Elizabeth. And one day he went down to Farfrae's yard and asked for a job. He was accepted at once.

"I have been a workman before now, haven't I?" he would say in his outspoken way. "And why shouldn't I be one again?"

At the beginning of winter, people were saying that Mr Farfrae would soon be Mayor.

"A fellow of his age going to be Mayor indeed!" said Henchard with a smile at the corner of his mouth. "It's her money that's pulling him upwards. Ha – how odd it is! Here am I that was his master, working for him as his man. And he is the man standing as master, with my house, and my furniture, and my what-you-may-call wife all his own."

He repeated these things a hundred times a day.

Elizabeth-Jane sat at her window one Sunday, and heard in the street below a conversation which introduced Henchard's name:

"Michael Henchard has burst out drinking after taking nothing for twenty-one years!"

One afternoon, the green side-door of Farfrae's house opened, and Lucetta came out into the yard. She came suddenly upon Henchard, who touched his hat to her like the other workmen.

She breathed a dead-and-alive "Good afternoon".

"Oh yes, good afternoon, ma'am," he replied, touching his hat again. "I am glad to see you, ma'am. We poor workmen here feel it a great honour that a lady should look in and take an interest in us."

She looked at him with her eyes asking for pity: his mood was too bitter, too hard to bear.

"Can you tell me the time, ma'am?" he asked.

"Yes," she said quickly. "Half-past four."

"Thank you. An hour-and-a-half longer before we are freed from our work. Ah, ma'am, we of the lower classes know nothing of the gay life that ladies like yourself enjoy!"

As soon as she could, Lucetta left him. Next morning, a note from her was put into Henchard's hand by the postman:

Will you kindly not speak to me in the biting manner you used today, if I walk through the yard at any time. I am very glad that you have employment of my dear husband. But in common fairness please treat me as his wife.

"Poor fool," said Henchard, and threw the letter into the fire.

Lucetta took care not to come again among the hay and the corn.

16

Farfrae had just got in from work, and the tea-kettle was singing, when Mr Vatt, a neighbour, called.

"You've heard I suppose of the death of Mr Chalkfield, the Mayor?" said Mr Vatt. "Died this afternoon at five."

Farfrae was sorry at the news, and Mr Vatt continued. "Well, we know he's been going for some days, so it's no surprise really. Now I have called to ask you this – quite privately. If I should put your name forward to take his place, and no one is against it, will you accept?"

"But there are folk whose turn is before mine. And I'm too young – people may not like it!" said Farfrae after a pause.

"Not at all. I don't speak for myself only.

Several have named you. You won't refuse?"

"Well, I would not refuse if it is the wish of the majority."

"Very well. Consider it done. We have had older men long enough."

From that evening onwards, Lucetta was very uneasy. She was so nervous that she spoke to Henchard when they met accidentally in the street a day or two later. It was at the busiest time in the market, when no one could easily notice their conversation.

"Michael," said she, "I must again ask you what I asked months ago – to return to me any letters or papers of mine that you have. What happened to them?"

He could not say – he said he would consider. When she had gone, he remembered that he had left a pile of useless papers in his dining-room safe, built up in the wall of his old house – now Farfrae's house. A curious smile shaped itself on Henchard's face. Had that safe been opened?

On the next evening there was a great ringing of bells in Casterbridge, and bands played round the town, with trumpets and drums even louder than usual. Farfrae was Mayor.

The next morning Henchard went to the corn-yard as usual, and about eleven o'clock Donald entered through the green door.

"I was going to ask you," said Henchard, "about a packet of papers that I may have left in my old safe in the dining-room."

"If so, it is there now," said Farfrae. "I have never opened the safe at all yet."

"It was not of much importance – to me," said Henchard. "But I'll call for it this evening, if you don't mind."

It was quite late when he called. He had filled himself up with beer, as he did very frequently now. Farfrae invited him into the dining-room, where he at once unlocked the iron safe. Farfrae took out the parcel, with apologies for keeping it so long.

"Never mind," said Henchard drily. "The fact is, they are letters mostly – yes." He went on, sitting down and unfolding the package of Lucetta's most private thoughts. "Here they are. I hope Mrs Farfrae is well."

"She felt a bit weary, and she's gone to bed early."

Henchard looked through the letters with interest. "You remember of course that curious part of my past that I told you about? These letters are related to that unhappy business."

"What became of the poor woman?" asked Farfrae.

"Luckily she married, and married well," said Henchard. "So all these complaints of hers.... Just listen to what an angry woman will say!"

Farfrae, though tired and quite uninterested, tried to show well-mannered concentration.

"For me," Henchard read, *"there is practically no future. I feel it impossible to be the wife of any other man — I am too deeply in love with you. Thus I sit here, forgotten by my few friends, and now forgotten by you!"*

"Yes," said Farfrae politely, "it is the way with women."

"That's how she went on," said Henchard. "Floods of words like that, about pains that I could not cure." He unfolded another letter and read it through. "Her name I don't give," he said innocently, "in fairness to her."

"But why didn't you marry her when your wife Susan died?" Farfrae asked, "She had already married another maybe?"

Henchard thought it better not to go further into details, and simply said, "Yes."

"The young lady must have been able to change her affections very easily then!"

"She did, she did!" said Henchard firmly.

He opened a third and fourth letter, and read. The truth was, he had meant to effect a grand disaster at the end, by reading out the name. He had come to the house with no other thought. But sitting there in Farfrae's house, he could not do it.

Such a wrecking of hearts was too much even for him.

17

Next evening when Lucetta was returning home, she saw a man waiting by the lamp nearest to her own door. It was Jopp.

"Beg pardon, ma'am," he said. "But I hear Mr Farfrae is looking for someone to join him in the business. I wish to offer myself, ma'am. I've already stated my qualifications to Mr Farfrae in a letter. But it would be a great help if you would put in a word in my favour."

"It is a thing I know nothing about," said Lucetta coldly.

"But you could be better witness to my good qualifications than anybody, ma'am," said Jopp. He added carefully, "I was in Jersey several years, and I knew you there by sight."

"Indeed," she replied, "but I knew nothing about you."

"Just think, ma'am – only a word or two from you. It would secure for me something I desire very much."

She refused to have anything to do with the affair, and left him on the pavement. Jopp watched her till she had disappeared, and then went home.

Henchard came down from his bedroom and said, "I wish you would do me a great favour, Jopp. Now, if you can. Leave this at Mrs Farfrae's for her. I should take it myself of course, but I don't wish to be seen there."

He handed Jopp a package in brown paper, then said goodnight and returned to his room. Jopp sat and stared at the packet. He knew there had been a warm relationship between Henchard and the now Mrs Farfrae. Jopp considered the matter.

Henchard had a parcel that belonged to Mrs

Farfrae, but he did not wish to return it himself. What could be inside it? Jopp thought about the parcel, and he thought about Mrs Farfrae's refusal to help him. The brown paper was stuck down, but Jopp took out a knife and lifted one of the edges. He could see that the package was a pile of letters. He pressed the edge down again and went off with the parcel.

His path was by the riverside at the foot of the town. At the bridge he met Mother Cuxsom and Nance Mockridge.

"We're just going down Mixen Lane," said Mrs Cuxson, "to look into Peter's Finger before going to bed. Do you come along too, Jopp. It won't keep you five minutes."

Without many words he agreed to go that way.

Mixen Lane was the hiding place of those who were in trouble of every kind. People in debt, workers who were too lazy to work, servants who refused to serve – they were all forced into Mixen Lane. Crime ran freely in and out of certain of its doors.

The public house called Peter's Finger was at the centre of Mixen Lane, and here Jopp and his friends had arrived. The furmity woman sat among the rest, and it was she who asked Jopp about the parcel under his arm.

"Ah, inside lies a great secret," said Jopp. "The burning fires of love."

"And what person is the subject of it, sir?"

"One that stands high in this town. I'd like to shame her, the proud piece of silk! And 'tis her love-letters that I've got here."

"Love-letters? Then let's hear them, good friend," said Mother Cuxsom.

By this time Jopp had passed his finger under the loose edge and unfastened the parcel. The letters fell out, and he picked one up here and there, and read them aloud. Soon Lucetta's secret was uncovered.

"Mrs Farfrae wrote that!" said Nance Mockridge. "And now she's given herself to another man!"

At this moment a stranger came through the door. "Is this the way to Casterbridge?" he asked.

"No, you've lost your way, friend. You should have kept along the main road."

"What place is this?" asked the stranger.

"A public house."

"Ah. Then wet your throats at my expense."

He was a middle-aged man, with hair and beard grey before their time. He had a broad and friendly face. He was dressed with a certain awkward richness – his coat and cap were furred – and in his hand he carried a small wooden case with brass fastenings. While he drank, the conversation returned to Jopp's parcel.

"I say," said Nance, "what a grand excuse for a skimmity-ride!"

"True," said Mrs Cuxsom. " 'Tis the best cause for a skimmity-ride I ever knew. And it ought not to be wasted. The last one in Casterbridge must have been ten years ago."

The stranger said, "What do they mean by a skimmity-ride?"

"O, sir," said the landlady, swinging her long

ear-rings, " 'tis a foolish word we use in these parts. 'Tis a thing we do when a man's wife is – well – not entirely his own."

"Are they going to do a skimmity? It's a good sight to see, I suppose?"

"Well, sir," she burst into sudden laughter, " 'tis the funniest thing under the sun! And it costs money."

"I shall be in Casterbridge for two or three weeks, I expect, and I should like to see the performance. Here, good folks, take that as a help towards it."

He threw a gold coin on the table, asked the way to the town, and left. Jopp gathered up the letters, fastened up the parcel, and delivered it at its address next morning.

Within an hour it was burnt to ashes by Lucetta. She fell down on her knees in thankfulness that no one could know her guilty secret.

18

As Farfrae came out through the green door, the low light of nearing evening caught his head and face, and warmed them to a flame-colour. He was dressed for a journey. He had just received an unsigned letter with the word *immediate* on the outside. The note contained a brief request that he go to Weatherbury that evening about some business.

Farfrae brought out a horse and light carriage, and set out on his way.

In fact this letter was a well-meaning but clumsy attempt by some of his men to get him out of the way for the evening. The skimmity-ride was planned for this evening, and it was directed at Lucetta, not at Farfrae.

It was about eight o'clock, and Lucetta was in the sitting-room alone. She had not lighted the candles, as she preferred to wait for Farfrae by firelight. She kept one of her windows open a little way, so that the sound of his wheels could reach her ears early.

It had been dark for half an hour when her thoughts were disturbed by a noisy crowd in the distance. Then she heard the voice of a maid-servant next door, speaking to some other maid at an upper window across the street.

"Which way are they going now?" inquired the first with interest.

"They're coming up from Corn Street," said the second. "They're sitting back to back!"

"What – are there two figures?"

"Yes. Two images on a donkey, back to back, their elbows tied to each other's! She's facing the head, and he's facing the tail."

"Who do they look like?"

"Well – the man has got on a blue coat. He has black hair and a reddish face. 'Tis a stuffed figure.

With a false face."

"What's the woman like? Is it meant for the one I have in mind?"

"Ah! 'Tis dressed just as *she* was dressed when she went to see the play-actors at the Town Hall!"

Lucetta jumped to her feet, and almost at the same moment the door of the room was quickly and softly opened. Elizabeth-Jane advanced into the firelight.

"I did not stop to knock – forgive me!" she said breathlessly.

Without waiting for Lucetta's reply, she crossed quickly to the window and closed the curtains. Lucetta came to her side, and the conversation outside continued.

"Her neck is uncovered, and her hair's in bands. She's got on a purple silk dress, and white stockings, and coloured shoes."

Elizabeth-Jane attempted to close the window, but Lucetta held her by main force.

" 'Tis me!" she said with a face as pale as death. "A procession – an image of me and a man!"

"Let us shut it out," said Elizabeth-Jane, "let us shut it out!"

"It's no use," Lucetta screamed out. "He will see it, won't he? Donald will see it! He's just coming home – and it will break his heart – he will never love me any more – and O, it will kill me, kill me!"

Elizabeth-Jane was badly alarmed now. "O, is there nobody to stop it?" she cried.

Lucetta herself shouted, "I will see it!"

She pulled the curtains aside and threw open

the window. Her eyes looked straight out on to the sight of the wild procession, now advancing rapidly. The numerous lights made the two images very clear: it was impossible to mistake the pair.

"Come in, come in," begged Elizabeth, "and let me shut the window!"

"She's me – she's me – even with my green umbrella!" cried Lucetta with a wild laugh.

She stood entirely still for one second – then fell heavily to the floor. Almost at the moment of her fall the noisy music of the skimmity-ride came to an end, and the roars of laughter died away.

Elizabeth had rung the bell for the servants, and was bending over Lucetta. A light was obtained, Lucetta was carried to her room, and someone sent off for the doctor.

As soon as he saw the unhappy sufferer, the doctor said, "You must send at once for Mr Farfrae. Where is he?"

"He has driven into the country, sir," said one of the maids. "He's likely to be back soon."

The doctor returned to the bedside.

"This is serious," he said.

Henchard had been walking towards the town when the procession burst into his view. He was surprised by the lamps, the horns, and the noisy crowds. He saw the images, and knew what it all meant.

The procession crossed the way, entered another street, and disappeared. He turned back a few steps and made his way homeward by the riverside path. Unable to rest there, he went to Elizabeth's rooms, and was told that she had gone to Mrs Farfrae's.

With a nameless fear in his heart, he followed in the same direction. He gave the gentlest of pulls to the doorbell, and then learnt what had happened.

"How is she?" Henchard asked Elizabeth.

"In great danger, father. Poor woman – I fear they have killed her."

Henchard stared at her for a few moments, then, without another word, he turned away and went back to his lonely cottage.

Jopp was just going to bed when Henchard got home. "Somebody has called for you," said Jopp. "A kind of traveller, or a sea-captain of some sort."

"Oh! – Who could he be?"

"He seemed quite a well-off kind of a man – grey hair and a broad face. But he gave me no name and no message."

"Then I give him no interest."

And Henchard closed the door.

It was almost two hours before Farfrae got home. When he had left, his wife had been a healthy woman, with his child inside her. Now she was seriously ill, and she had lost the baby. He seldom left her side that night, and she tried to whisper to him the secret that she had hidden all these years.

Henchard's night was also without rest. He gave up attempts at sleep, and called to make inquiries about the patient every now and then.

The last of his calls was made about four o'clock in the morning, in the steely light of dawn. The door was gently opened, and a servant began to untie the piece of cloth that had deadened the sound of the door-knocker.

"Why do you take off that?" said Henchard.

It was a moment or two before she recognised him. Then she said, "Because they may knock as loud as they wish: she will never hear it any more."

19

Henchard went home. He lit his fire and sat beside it with his heart empty of all feeling. A gentle footstep approached the house and entered the passage, and a finger tapped lightly at the door. Henchard's face brightened, because he knew that the movements were Elizabeth's.

"Have you heard?" she asked. "Mrs Farfrae. She is – dead!"

"I know it," said Henchard. "It is very good of you, Elizabeth, to come and tell me. You must be tired out, too, after sitting up all night. Now you stay here with me this morning. You can go and rest in the other room. I'll call you when breakfast's ready."

She went into the next room and lay down. For a while she heard him moving about in his preparations. Then she fell asleep.

Henchard soon had the breakfast ready, but when he found her asleep he would not call her. He looked into the fire, and kept the kettle boiling for her, as if it was an honour to have her in his house. In truth he was developing a dream of a future lit by her presence.

He was disturbed by a knock at the door, and rose to open it. A well-built man stood on the doorstep. It was the man who had asked the way at Peter's Finger.

"Good morning, good morning," said the stranger with great cheerfulness. "Is it Mr Henchard I am talking to?"

"My name is Henchard."

"You may remember me? My name is Newson."

Henchard's face and eyes seemed to die. "I know the name well," Henchard said at last, and showed the way in.

"Well, I've been looking for you these past two weeks. 'He lives down by the mill,' they said. So here I am. Now – that business between us some twenty years ago. That's what I've called about," said Newson. "Poor Susan. You know that your child died, and she had another?"

Henchard nodded.

"Susan was a simple woman. She believed I was her rightful husband, because of the payment. But then somebody told her our 'marriage' was

91

not lawful, and people made a joke of it. After that she was never happy with me, and she just sighed and sighed.

"So I left her at Falmouth, and went off to sea. At the other side of the Atlantic, some of us were washed overboard. I thought, 'If she thinks I'm dead, she'll go back to him, and the child will have a home.'

"I've never returned to this country till a month ago. They told me in Falmouth that Susan was dead. But my Elizabeth-Jane – how is she?"

"Also dead," said Henchard solidly.

The sailor jumped up. "Dead!" he said in a low voice. "Then what's the use of my money to me? Where is she buried?"

"Beside her mother," said Henchard.

"When did she die?"

"A year ago and more," replied the other, with his eyes on the floor.

At last Newson said, "My journey here has been for nothing! I may as well go as I came! I'll trouble you no longer."

Henchard heard the retreating footsteps, and the slow opening and closing of the door. Newson's shadow passed the window. He was gone.

Henchard hardly believed the evidence of his senses, and he rose from his seat, amazed at what he had done. The words had come from him unplanned, a result of a sudden fear that he would lose Elizabeth.

He quickly put on his hat and went out, and followed Newson. The coach that had brought

Newson was now about to move again. Newson climbed on board, and his luggage was put in. In a few minutes the coach disappeared with him.

He had not even turned his head. It was an act of simple trust in Henchard's words. When Henchard returned to his house, Elizabeth was just coming out from the inner room, with the marks of sleep upon her eyelids.

"O father," she said smiling, "it is so kind of you to get this nice breakfast with your own hands."

"I do it every day," he replied. "You have left me: everybody has left me. How should I live except by my own hands?"

"You are very lonely, are you not?"

"Yes, child. It is my own fault. You are the only one who has been near me for weeks. And you will come no more."

"Why do you say that? Father! – I will not leave you alone like this!" she cried. "May I live with you and look after you as I used to do? I do not mind your being poor."

"*May* you come to me?" he cried bitterly. "Elizabeth, don't make fun of me! If only you *would* come!"

"I will," said she.

"How will you forgive all my roughness of earlier days? You cannot!"

"I have forgotten it. Talk of that no more."

She returned to her rooms. Then Henchard shaved for the first time during many days, and put on clean clothes, and combed his hair.

20

Lucetta had been carried along the churchyard path, and Casterbridge went about its work as if she had never lived. Elizabeth now shared Henchard's home. He swallowed his pride and accepted a small seed and root business that Farfrae and the Town Hall had bought for him. Thus Henchard and Elizabeth lived in the shop that looked out on the churchyard.

Lucetta had confessed everything to Farfrae before her death. In time he had learned of the skimmity-ride, and he realised that he had exchanged a lifetime of unhappiness for a simple sorrow.

By the end of a year the little seed and grain shop – not much larger than a cupboard – had developed its trade considerably. Henchard and Elizabeth enjoyed great peace in the pleasant, sunny corner where it stood.

Henchard let her have her own way in everything now. In going and coming, in buying and selling, her word was law.

"You have got some new gloves, Elizabeth," he said to her one day. "Rather costly, I suppose, my dear, were they not?"

"They were rather above my price," she said quietly. "But they are not too showy."

"O no," said the tame lion, anxious not to annoy her in the least.

The year advanced into another spring, and the busy time of the seed trade was over. The quiet weeks before the hay season had come, and the market was crowded with new carts in yellow and green and red.

Henchard went out 'one Saturday afternoon towards the market-place. Farfrae stood a few steps below the Corn Exchange door: he appeared to be lost in thought about something a little way off. Henchard's eyes followed Farfrae's, and saw that the object of his interest was not a trading farmer, but Elizabeth-Jane.

From now on, Henchard became uneasy at the thought of a love for Farfrae that could displace her feelings towards himself. He watched her comings and goings more narrowly.

Elizabeth-Jane began to take long walks in the country two or three times a week. At the time of her return from those walks on the Budmouth Road, Donald often left Corn Street, to wander for twenty minutes along the same rather winding highway.

Henchard became aware of this by going to the Ring, and keeping his eyes on the road till he saw them meet. They went along the road together till they reached the town, and their paths separated. Henchard swore to himself that he would not interfere, but he continued to watch with anxiety.

Then one day, from behind a wall, he heard the young man address her as 'dearest Elizabeth-Jane', and then kiss her.

When they had gone on their way, Henchard sadly followed them to Casterbridge.

About three kilometres from the town, and less than a kilometre from the Budmouth Road, there stood a huge and ancient fort. From here it became Henchard's habit to examine the road through a telescope and watch the progress of affairs between Farfrae and his young lady-love.

One day a male figure came along the road from Budmouth and stopped. Henchard placed the telescope to his eye, but it showed him that today the man was not Elizabeth-Jane's lover. It was someone clothed as a sea-captain. Henchard lived a lifetime, the moment he saw the face – it was Newson's. Henchard waited and Newson waited, but Elizabeth-Jane did not come that morning. When Henchard reached his own house, he found her there.

"O father!" she said innocently, "I've had a letter – a strange one – not signed. Somebody has asked me to meet him, either on the Budmouth Road at noon today, or in the evening at Mr Farfrae's. He says he came to see me some time ago, but a trick was played on him, so that he did not see me. I don't understand it. But I did not like to go till I had seen you. Shall I go?"

Henchard replied heavily, "Yes." Then he surprised the young woman by saying to her, "I am going to leave Casterbridge, Elizabeth-Jane."

"Leave Casterbridge!" she cried, "and leave me?"

"Yes. You can manage this little shop alone as well as both of us. I would rather go into the country by myself, out of sight, and follow my own ways, and leave you to yours."

She looked down and the tears fell silently.

"I am sorry you have decided on this," she said with difficulty. "I thought it probable – possible – that I might marry Mr Farfrae, and I did not know that you disapproved."

"I approve of everything you desire to do, Elizabeth-Jane," said Henchard softly. "But my presence might make things awkward for you in the future. In short, it is best that I go."

"Then," she said at last, "you will not be able to come to my wedding."

"I don't want to see it – I don't want to see it!" he cried, and added more softly, "But think of me sometimes. Promise not to quite forget me when...." He meant when Newson came.

That evening at dusk Henchard left the town. During the day he had bought a new tool-basket, cleaned up his old hay-knife, and gone back to the working clothes of his young manhood. He went secretly and alone. Elizabeth-Jane went with him as far as the second bridge on the highway, and then watched his form grow smaller in the distance.

When she returned, Donald was waiting for her. She went into his house, and Farfrae threw open the door of the sitting-room, saying, "There

97

he is, waiting for you."

In the armchair sat the broad-faced, friendly man who had called on Henchard more than a year before. The meeting between father and daughter need hardly be described. It was a joyful one, and the reason for Henchard's departure was immediately clear. Newson kissed her again and again.

"Well, Captain Newson," said Farfrae, "I will be glad to see you here every day now."

"With all my heart," said Captain Newson. "And it can do no harm, now that poor Henchard's gone."

For the first time Donald and Elizabeth-Jane learned of Henchard's trick when Newson had visited Casterbridge before.

"You are always so trusting, father," said Elizabeth-Jane. "I've heard my mother say so hundreds of times. And he wronged you. He should not have done that."

"Well, well – never mind – it is all over and past," said Newson good-naturedly. "Now, about this wedding!"

21

Henchard went his lonely way eastwards till weariness overtook him, and he looked about for a place to rest. He could not get Elizabeth out of his mind, and he was so full of sorrow that he could not bear to look for a house.

He lay down in a wheat-field, uninterested in food. The heaviness of his heart caused him to sleep deeply.

The bright autumn sun awoke him early next morning, and he opened his basket, and ate the supper of the night before. Among his tools lay a few of Elizabeth's belongings – gloves, shoes, a few words of her handwriting. And in his pocket he carried a piece of her hair. He looked at these things and closed them up again, then went onwards.

For five days Henchard's basket rode along upon his shoulder. He meant to go far away into another part of the country, but he could not help thinking of Elizabeth. As a result, he did not follow a straight course further away from Casterbridge, but came gradually round in a circle.

And he said to himself, "O, you fool! All this

about a daughter who is no daughter of yours!"

As it was autumn time, he easily found work for his hay-knife, and chose a farm near the old western highway. He often kept an eager ear upon the conversation of those who passed along the road, and one day he heard the name 'Casterbridge' from the lips of a cart-driver.

"Yes, I've come from there," he said, in answer to Henchard's inquiry.

"Anything moving in the old place, may I ask?"

"All the same as usual."

"Maybe you know Mr Farfrae, who was once Mayor. I've heard that he's thinking of getting married. Now is that true or not?"

"I couldn't say. O no, I should think not."

"But yes, John – you forget," said a woman in the cart. "You remember those packages we carried there at the beginning of the week? Surely they said there'd be a wedding soon – on the eleventh of November, wasn't it?"

The man said he remembered nothing about it, and the cart went on over the hill.

Henchard was sure that the woman's memory served her well. The date was a very probable one, as there was no reason for delay. He had been certain that Newson would return. *And* that Elizabeth-Jane would welcome him. *And* that if Newson returned, he would stay. Supposing Henchard was mistaken in his views?

It was worth the risk to make one more attempt to be near her – to go back – to ask her forgiveness. He worked for two days more, then he suddenly decided to go to the wedding. He did not wish to force himself upon the company and spoil the happy event, so he decided not to appear till evening.

He possessed no clothes except his working suit, and that was now dirty and dusty. He entered a shop and bought a new coat and hat, and a new shirt and neck-cloth. Next he turned his mind to a wedding-present.

He walked up and down the street, looking in the shop windows. At last a caged bird met his eye – a bird with a pretty red-and-white face, and golden bars across its wings. The cage was a plain and small one, and Henchard decided he could afford the price. He tied a sheet of newspaper round the little creature's wire prison, and next day he set out on the three-day walk to Casterbridge.

It was just after twelve o'clock when he came in sight of the town, and the soft ringing of the bells told him that all had gone well: Elizabeth-Jane and Donald Farfrae were man and wife. He passed the remainder of the afternoon in the fields beside the highway. Then he dusted his boots, washed his hands at the riverside, and went into town under the newly-lit lamps.

When he came near to Farfrae's house, it was plain that a great party was going on inside. The door was wide open, the hall was brightly lit, and people were going up and down the stairs.

Henchard's courage failed him, poorly dressed as he was. So he went round to the back and entered the garden, and came quietly into the house through the kitchen. For the moment he left

the bird and cage under a bush outside.

There was only an elderly woman in the kitchen, and when Henchard asked to see the bride and bridegroom, she took him up into a little back room, which was empty. Here she left him. She said that she would have a word with Mr and Mrs Farfrae when the dance had finished.

Across the passage Henchard could see the dancers through the partly-closed door. They flew past, with spinning skirts and dresses, and streaming hair.

Then Henchard caught sight of Elizabeth-Jane, and it made his heart ache. She was in a dress of snowy white silk. She was dancing with someone who was turning grandly round, his head shaking up and down, his legs in the form of an X, and his back towards the door. The next time, he came round in the other direction. That happy face belonged to Newson, who had indeed come and taken Henchard's place.

Henchard rose to his feet and prepared to leave. But the dance ended, and Elizabeth-Jane entered the room immediately.

"Oh – it is – Mr Henchard!" she said in surprise and confusion.

"What, Elizabeth," he cried, as he seized her hand. "What do you say? – *Mr Henchard?* Don't be as cold as this! I see you have a real father in my place. But save some thought for me!"

She gently took her hand away, "I could have loved you always. But you kept me from my warm-hearted real father. You cruelly sent him away and told him I was dead, which nearly broke his heart. How can I love a man who has served us like this!"

His lips opened to begin an explanation, but he shut them again and breathed not a sound.

"Don't upset yourself because of me," he said proudly. "I would not wish it – and at such a time as this, too. I have done wrong in coming to you – I see that. But it is only for once, so forgive it. I'll never trouble you again, Elizabeth-Jane. Good-night, goodbye!"

Then before she could gather her thoughts, Henchard went out from her rooms, and departed from the house by the back way again.

She saw him no more.

22

It was about a month after the wedding-day. Newson had stayed in Casterbridge for three days after the wedding party. On the fourth morning someone saw him sadly climbing a hill, trying to catch sight of the sea from somewhere. He went off to stay in Budmouth, in a cottage where he could see a band of blue sea from the open window.

Elizabeth-Jane was in an upstairs room of her house when a maid came in and said, "Oh please, ma'am, we know now how the birdcage came there."

During the first week of her marriage, Mrs Donald Farfrae had been exploring the garden, when she discovered a new birdcage. It was covered in newspaper, and at the bottom of the cage was a little ball of feathers – the dead body of a bird. No one could tell her where the little singer had come from. The sadness of it had affected her deeply, and she was not able to forget it for days.

"Oh please, ma'am, we know how the birdcage came there. That farmer's man who called on the evening of the wedding – he was seen with it in his hand as he came up the street. He must have put it down when he came in with his message. Then he forgot where he'd left it."

Elizabeth realised immediately that Henchard had brought the bird as a wedding gift for her. Her heart softened towards the lonely man, and she begged Donald to help her find him. She wanted to make her peace with him, to make life more bearable for him.

But Henchard had disappeared. Farfrae made inquiries in the town. Someone had seen Henchard walking along the Melchester highway. This was enough, and Farfrae drove off in his light carriage, with Elizabeth-Jane sitting beside him, wrapped in a thick fur.

After a few kilometres they met a roadmender who had been working there for some weeks. He had seen such a man who left the Melchester coach road at Weatherbury, and took the highway that went north of Egdon Heath.

Into this road they directed the horse's head. They searched Egdon, but found no Henchard.

Farfrae advised his wife to give up the search. They were now at least thirty kilometres from home. If they rested the horse for a couple of hours, they could get back to Casterbridge that same day.

While they waited, a human form came from under the trees and crossed ahead of them. His walk was slow and awkward, and in his hand he carried a few sticks of firewood. After he crossed the road, he went into a cottage.

"If we were in Casterbridge, I would say that was poor Abel Whittle. It is just like him," said Elizabeth-Jane.

"And it may be Whittle – he's not been to my yard these three weeks, and I owe him for two days work."

Farfrae tied the horse to the gatepost, and they went up to the poor little cottage. There were holes in the roof, and leaves had been blown in the corners of the doorway.

Farfrae knocked at the half-open door, and the man who stood before them was indeed Whittle. His face showed marks of deep sadness. As soon as he saw them, his eyes lit up with surprise.

"What Abel Whittle? Is it really you?" said Farfrae.

"Ah, yes sir. You see – he was kind to my poor mother when she lived."

"Who are you talking of?"

"O, sir – Mr Henchard!"

"What of him?" said Elizabeth quickly.

"Didn't you know it? He's just gone – about half an hour ago by the sun."

"Not – dead?" whispered Elizabeth-Jane.

"Yes, ma'am. He's gone. Kind to my old mother, he was. Used to send her the best coal, and potatoes, when she was badly ill. The night of your wedding, sir, I saw Mr Henchard go down the street, and I thought he looked low and in need of help.

"I followed him over Grey's Bridge. And he turned and saw me and said, 'You go back. Do you hear, sir? Go back!' But I followed still. Then he said, 'Whittle, why do you follow me when I've told you to go back all these times?' And I said, 'Because, sir, I can see things are bad with you. And you were kind to my dear mother, sir, and I wish to be kind to you.'

"Then he walked on and I followed, and we walked on like that all night. And in the blue of the morning, I saw that he could hardly creep along. By that time we had got here, and I saw that this house was empty. I took down the boards from the windows, and helped him inside.

" 'What, Whittle,' he said, 'can you really be such a fool as to care for a worthless creature like me!'

"I made him as comfortable as I could. But he didn't gain strength, ma'am, because you see, ma'am, he couldn't eat – and he just got weaker. And today he died."

Elizabeth said nothing.

"Upon the head of his bed he pinned a piece of paper, with some writing on it," continued Abel

108

Whittle. "But I can't read writing, so I don't know what it says. I can get it and show you."

They stood in silence while he ran into the cottage. In a moment he returned with a crushed piece of paper. As Elizabeth-Jane looked at the words, she said through her tears, "O Donald! What bitterness lies here! If only I had not been so unkind at that last party.... But there's no changing it now – so it must be!"

On the paper were these words in pencil:

MICHAEL HENCHARD'S WILL

I wish that Elizabeth-Jane Farfrae be not told of my death, and that she is not made to sorrow because of me. I wish also —
that I be not buried in holy ground
that no bells are rung for me
that nobody see my dead body
that no flowers be planted on my grave
and that no man remember me.
To this I put my name.

MICHAEL HENCHARD

A Crossword

When you've finished this crossword, read the letters from one corner to another. You'll find the name of something or someone that helped the Mayor of Casterbridge.
Good luck!

1		2		3	4		5	6	7	8
	9		10							
11			12	13						
14			15			16				
17		18			19			20		
	21						22			
	23		24					25		
26			27	28				29	30	31
3		33				34		35		
	36									
	37					38				

Across

1 Elizabeth first saw Henchard at the King's
   _____.(4)
3 Lucetta lived at High-_____Hall. (5)
9 Henchard thought he would be a_____father
   than Newson. (6)
11 Fasten. (3)
12 When wheat prices went up, Donald sold his
   _____supply. (6)
14 Paintings and drawings. (3)
15 Jopp took Lucetta's to Peter's Finger. (7)
18 Elizabeth's father. (6)
20 Just before Henchard died, he was_____ill to
   eat. (3)

110

21 Henchard owed most of his ____ to Grower. (4)
23 Henchard: "I ____ so bad at letters." (2)
24 A mayor wears a gold one. (5)
25 Both of Elizabeth-Jane's were grey. (3)
26 Henchard's was 21 when Susan left him. (3)
27 There was only one case in the magistrates' court: an ____ woman in ancient clothes. (3)
29 Susan searched for the furmity woman, to ____ about Michael. (3)
32 Lucetta went to Port-Bredy to ____ married. (3)
34 When Henchard woke up in the tent, ____ found Susan's wedding ring. (2)
35 Heavy weight. (3)
36 The end of your leg. (3)
37 Henchard stayed at his cottage. (4)
38 Rescued. (5)

Down
1 Do something! (3)
2 "____ me at 8 o'clock this evening." (4)
4 In the seed shop, Henchard ____ Elizabeth have her own way in everything. (3)
5 Henchard took ____ not to annoy Elizabeth in any way. (4)
6 "He swore never to have strong drink, and he's kept to his promise ____ since." (4)
7 Something to learn. (6)
8 The furmity woman was at the fair here. (6)
9 After Elizabeth's wedding, it was found in the garden. (8)
10 Henchard began to watch the Budmouth Road through one. (9)

13 Henchard bought a ____ hat and coat, to go to Elizabeth's wedding. (3)
16 Late today. (7)
17 Donald took a job as Henchard's____. (7)
18 At Donald's marriage, the witness's ____ was Grower. (4)
19 Henchard hid in these to avoid meeting Donald and Lucetta in the shaded avenue. (7)
20 The Ring had been a Roman open-air ____. (7)
22 Come in! (5)
28 Jopp waited for Lucetta beside a street ____. (4)
30 Henchard ____ his wife for five pounds. (4)
31 Part of your leg. (4)
33 When Farfrae went to the Three Sailors, Susan and Elizabeth went there ____. (3)

Answers

Across

1 Arms 3 Place 9 better 11 tie
12 entire 14 art 15 letters 18 Newson
20 too 21 cash 23 am 24 chain 25 eye
26 age 27 old 29 ask 32 get 34 he 35 ton
36 toe 37 Jopp 38 saved

Down

1 act 2 meet 4 let 5 care 6 ever
7 lesson 8 Weydon 9 birdcage
10 telescope 13 new 16 tonight
17 manager 18 name 19 shadows
20 theatre 22 enter 28 lamp 30 sold
31 knee 33 too